DOOR = JAR

Door Is A Jar
Issue 17

www.doorisajarmagazine.net

3

Editors

Maxwell Bauman, Editor-in-Chief/ Art Director

Jack Fabian, Managing Editor/ Nonfiction Editor

Nina Long, Fiction Editor

Corrine Nulton, Poetry Editor/ Drama Editor

Cover Image "Royal Turkey"
by June Levitan

Table of Contents

A Fair Amount of Ghosts
Zach Murphy
Fiction

He plays the trumpet brilliantly on the corner of Grand and Victoria. He doesn't look like he's from this era. He's impeccably dressed, from his crisply fitting suit to his smooth fedora hat. There aren't many folks that can pull that off. He's cooler than the freezer aisle on a sweltering summer day. He performs the type of yearning melodies that give you the goosebumps. I've never seen anyone put any money into his basket.

There's a formidable stone house that sits atop Fairmount Hill. It's been for sale for as long as I can remember. The crooked post sinks deeper into the soil with each passing year. It isn't a place to live in. It's a place to dwell in. There's a dusty rocking chair on the front porch. It's always rocking. Always rocking. I'm not sure if the chair is occupied by an old soul or if it's just the wind. Maybe it's both. I guess the wind is an old soul.

This town is full of posters for Missing Cats. There's one for a sweet, fluffy Maine Coon named "Bear." He's been gone for a while now. I've searched through every alleyway, under every porch, and inside of every bush for him. Sometimes I think I see him out of the corner of my eye. But then he's not there. The rain has pretty much washed away the tattered posters. If he ever turns up, I worry that the posters will be missing.

I met the love of my life in Irvine Park, near the gloriously spouting water fountain, beneath the serene umbrella of oak trees. We spent a small piece of eternity there together. We talked about whether or not the world was coming to an end soon, and if all of our memories will be diminished along with it. After we said our goodbyes and she walked off into the distance, I never saw her again. So I left my heart in Irvine Park.

Sky Sailing
Rami Obeid
Poetry

It is unfair to everyone
That I would want to stay up here forever
Because the sights are far too beautiful,
To ever want to come back down

I sail through the clouds during my reign,
While it rains down on earth
I am above all that
And nothing can touch me up here

My boat is made up of old receipts,
And cheap plastic
These things never leave my pockets;
Because I carry them everywhere

And when I sail through the sky,
On the border of black and blue
I am alone because I am selfish
I want this for no one else but myself

My notebook keeps getting wet from vapor
And so I write words in the sky

Strange Terrain
Anthony Salandy
Poetry

As cobbled streets
Gave way to urban alleys
And tarmac highways

I found myself lost
In the strange terrain
Of a world so empty —

That the loud risings
Of individuals so encapsulated
In their personal worlds

Became merely a silence
That grew to overcome
Any sense of collectivity

Amongst the discontented masses,
For I was alone in a microcosmic world
So devoid of companionship

That even as pedestrians crowded
There was an isolation
So striking that the hollow buildings-

Served as my only reality
Amongst the rational world
So bureaucratic that any semblance

Of emotion became just an algorithm
Or recording just like any other,
In a world where distanciation —

Gave me assurance of cyber contact
As a security for the slow waning
Emotional sensitivity which consumed me,

Deep in the strange terrain of modern society.

Vacation's End
Michael Farfel
Fiction

Desert all around, dust and hill spire and dots of antelope. A family of four ride the highway West. Old car. Oldish father, mother. Two children in the backseat. The daughter clamors to the window. Nostril imprint, blue-purple lips.

"Can't we stop?" she near cries.

The father huffs.

Her brother repeats the question.

The mother turns. Black tired ringlets spattered across her brow. She doesn't speak — they cower.

Powerlines ghost by in twos and the siblings can't help but point. Whisper communications about how they'd climb the distant giants. The mother calls them twins. They're not. The son is black-haired, twisty-curly, fat-nosed, bone-jawed. The daughter is fair-eyed, fair-skinned. The father has joked, They can't be mine — are they the milkman's, the roofer's?

He's not joking now. He's dead on home. Floored, 80-90-95. The car struggles and speaks—fan belt clucking, suspension cussing. Age old rust sparks and dusts the road behind them.

"Music?" he asks.

They are beautiful, man and wife. But now, their voyage home, they look like drench-soaked sailors, undrunk. Filled gills with sand and salt. Vacationers who are vacationed out. She is tall and scrunched in her seat — long, oaky, sweaty legs cross and uncross. A tick of nervousness, a tick of *going too fast*. She adjusts her bunched up dress in fidgets — yellow flowers, brown and black. He is long too; his kids think of him as bendy, angular, a limber-looking willow tree.

The scenery scrubs by. Spacecraft-like. Windows cracked open, rushed air smell, huzzary buzzary. Mountains in the distance, flattop, once bedrock, shift and adjust the horizon. The children watch the passing sunlight shape the plains. Shadowed creatures manifest and bound through the orange-waveryness.

The mother tries the radio. Crackle, crackcrickle. Drums, bassline, high note, for a moment. Cawcurring, cawcrackle, currcaw. Father shakes his head no. "Worth a shot," he mouths and puts his full weight into the steering wheel. He's no longer ending, but bending and formed to the helm. Faded leather clutched, atomic level binding. Man is car is man.

Silhouetted on the side of the road an arch of rock rises. The children jostle in their seats and dare another, "Please?"

"No," father blurts.

"But..."

He turns to face them. Wild white slit wide-eyed eyes, red. Car is man is. Floating now. Steady, steady. Screeching. Steel buckling. Correction. Bucking bronco. Uncorrected. Gored through matador. Concussive, coconuts. Yelping. Screaming. Howling. Full earful, full near death. Full tilting. One way, one way.

Silence.

The car, the wife, the husband, the two children, all frozen in debris and rising dust, all breathing deeply, all checking for pulses and lost body parts. The mother speaks first, but makes no sense, an incomprehensible syllable, syllable, sob. The father peels his hands from the wheel and laughs. The car is dead; mangled, hissing. The children tumble out. Unafraid. In fact, the blood on the son's forehead makes them giddy. The daughter touches it with the fat of her hand and presses it to her face. Palm printed beauty.

Purpling leviathans, born in the up-dripping dusk, surround them — their shadows stretch and fill the world with trick light. Moon rising wind noise whistles and groans and grows in echoes as the children dance. Holding hands and cheering in their freedom. The red earth pales yellow.

Gray clouds gather, orange-lined. Lightning in their hollows. Mother and father sit quietly in the wreckage, a moment of reprieve. She reaches across the console and touches his face. Stubbled, new-wrinkled, still young-eyed. She follows his jawline to pink lip line to temples. Curled silver over his sweat-peaked ears. His calloused hand rests above her bare knee and walks, mandolinlike, up her thigh. Smoke smell and binding piston reek can't stop them. Tooth tongue, lip stumbling, never alone, alone at last.

The children make it to the near hills — have gathered sticks and rocks, rubies and diamonds; new friends, wolves and birds. Volcanic black rocks, in slips and slabs, crunch under their feet as they climb. They hold their hands in binocular shape and stake claims on all creation. Nightfall covers the earth. Thunder amasses, east and west. Headwinds collide headwinds. Dust devils. Devils. Darkness. Will be mine, the children say. And mine and mine.

Lonely shadow of memories
Awósùsì Olúwábùkúnmí Abraham
Poetry

My body is like a desolated
chapel — echoing the memories of candlelights
and fragile shadows.

One does not value the essence of life
until it began to slip away in whistling moments
and play back in recurring memories
in the confinement of oneself.

And on these days when
death has outcast humans to the silence of their room;
my body, an echoing house of memories
lit up the candle light in the chapel
and once again, revisit these memories of lonely
shadows.

Examples of Confusion
Awósùsì Olúwábùkúnmí Abraham
Poetry

Our living room smells of memories,
of blood
of fights
of tears.

My mother dropped dead there yesterday
perhaps I am hallucinating.

& when I woke up this morning,
she had a smile on her face like that of
a little girl.

the moon is a language that speaks of silent memories
Awósùsì Olúwábùkúnmí Abraham
Poetry

we do not know what it means
as we sat in the woods.
you said you love to hunt butterflies because they are
beautiful. i said i prefer to stare at the moon.
even though we both know that the moon is fueled by
memories of those who are lost to silence.
we called it love
as we kissed under the watching moonlight —
but the rest are histories,
& as i walk the wood this night
the moon shines brighter with memories silently
sealed off in my lonely body.

The Searchers
Brett Biebel
Fiction

I spent the summer visiting dead places. Effigy Mounds
and the Buddy Holly crash site and some nothing
Nebraska nowhere with cars stacked up like Stonehenge.
It looked reasonably exact. In Utah, I met a Mormon on
the side of the road, and he had green eyes and wore a
full suit, and we drove to St. George while he talked
forever about radiation. Thyroid cancer. Wind patterns
and exposure lawsuits and labyrinthine acts of Congress,
and he said John Wayne died out here. "Not exactly," he
said. "But cells are a time bomb, and this is the place
that started his clock."

"It's beautiful," I said.

"You just have to know how to look." There were
canyons and megachurches, and everything seemed red.
Red rocks. Red sky. Red clouds. For a minute I thought
it was Mars. I dropped him on the steps of the
courthouse, and "Go on now," he said. "Ride them
highways and preach," and I had no idea what he meant,
but that's exactly what I did. I bought 12 copies of the
Book of Mormon and figured maybe I'd cruise 15 and
hit the Strip. Live Hollywood. The Pacific. Or maybe I'd
drive out to the Nevada Test Site and take one of the
tours, and maybe I'd sneak off. Find some quiet spot and
bury myself in the dirt and then just nibble on it, just put
it in my pockets and lug it around and let it breathe
through my skin, and this is how you become a man, I
thought. This is a Western. It's as close as you'll ever
get to John Marion Morrison Wayne.

Saving People
Heather Robinson
Fiction

We're a one religion family (atheism), we're a one parent family (me), we're a one kid family (Cherie), and we're a one income family (Cherie's only five, so I told her she's got a few more years of freedom). There's nothing to cushion us if I get sick, so, yes, I'm stressed, because I'm living in reality. At least I have Cherie, who is keeping me alive with her ridiculous antics. Yesterday when I picked her up from Little Cherubs she did a credible cover of *Someone You Loved,* even picking up some of that Scottish accent.

Then there's my friend Julie. She's is in a cult — well, I'm calling it that. The "NOT New Jesus Church" is another name I call it. She got "saved" two years ago. She was more fun before. Anyway, she's not really better off than I am because they're taking all her money and promising that she won't get sick if she goes to services there three times a week. I'm so tired of hearing her talk about it (on the phone people, I'm not crazy). She manages to pivot even normal conversations towards her church, even stupid things like how to make that French Toast Grilled Cheese sandwich. Yup, she actually told me that her pastor invented it.

Meanwhile, I just plug along trying to be a worthy successor to the great Ms. Nightingale. I'm only 38 but I've seen many lifetimes of pain and suffering. It's my obvious aim to help heal my patients. That's why I became a nurse and no matter what I do, I can't seem to switch it off. But there are days when I wonder. Like when DJ Planck shows up on a gurney for the umpteenth time, bleeding internally after his 211th bender in the midst of this catastrophe. Would Flo look at that ashen face and think, "this one is worth saving?" I don't know. Probably she would.

Speaking of saving people, there's no way for me to save Julie at this point. She's too deep in. Of course I'm worried for her, but frankly more focused on my own issues, like how to get an egg somewhere to make a French Toast Grilled Cheese sandwich for Cherie, who saw it on YouTube at daycare and now insists she'll die if she doesn't get one.

A Good Day at Pacific Beach
Linda Conroy
Poetry

Half way up the house
a splash of calla lilies
brilliant against grey weathered wood.

These fine white trumpets rise
in coastal wind, embrace the mist,
display their purity, their innocence.

Road travelers, children,
hikers on the sand, gasp, open-mouthed,
delighted with this gift.

Short Circuited
Linda Conroy
Poetry

He met her and he tumbled fast,
overcome by fascination
with her wit, her tender voice,
the way her fingers touched his cheek
when he held her coat and moved in close
as she slipped into it.

Taut desperation
dug roots into his hope, held tight,
as bliss bubbled, spread.
Delighted when she looked at him
as though she'd never look at someone else,
distraught, dismantled, when she did.

He told himself she couldn't help the way she was.
He'd love her better than the others would,
be her steadfastness, a buttress for her fall,
until she left. She would, he knew,
as if her hand could tip
dream's logic from his grasp.

Gift of a Sparrow's Nest
Sally Sandler
Poetry

It's like a present found under the tree
when everyone's sound asleep
on Christmas Eve, and the
thrill of trespassing.

The rustic wrapping is full of hope,
a family's intimate history written
in twisted straw and cursive grass
and sometimes fine sepia print.

There's the urgency of architecture:
this twig here, then this one
crossed with that one
just so, and a piece of dried leaf,

the inside saved for certain grass
as fine as human hair, neat and
sculpted as the mother's breast,
and at the center: her luminous eggs.

Here is the brief imprint of life.
The wonder of a mother bird's
skills, all the timing just right,
her chicks' complete belief

that their grim orange beaks
would be filled and they
would persist as surely
as mornings in May.

Third Eye
Rosie Sandler
Poetry

She took his eye with her
— said it gave her a different perspective.
She kept it in a tub of cold cream;
wiped it off when needed;
held it aloft — a gruesome chestnut,
eyeballing a shrunken view of the world.

She laughed when I asked
how he did without it.
You can ask him yourself if you like.
And she showed me his heart in a jar.

Still
Mark J. Mitchell
Poetry

Flat. Still. Resting on her perfect back while
she dreams cracks in her unscarred ceiling,
her stories stay the same. Her neighbors smile
and walk quickly by. She smiles back, brain reeling
with last night's dream. That long, slow, still mile
to her day job unrolls and God's words glow
behind her eyes. Desks. Duties. That tall pile
of laundry won't vanish. Her heart's kneeling
and no one sees. Your numb mouth wants to repeat
what night taught her. Still, they don't want to hear
a message she could bring. She's the un-neat
crazy lady, she knows. It costs no tears.
She sees, still, what's shown. The embracing glow's
her only pay. She is still. She's complete.

Late Surrealist
Mark J. Mitchell
Poetry

First, his fish wouldn't start.
It coughed out tiny diamonds
the precise color of her eyes.

He ran for a public balloon
but it floated off as he reached
the only cracked pyramid nearby.

Walking along Pudding Street.
shoes covered in lovely butterscotch,
he couldn't make time behave.

When two snakes hissed open
he tangoed — solo — to his desk
to find a lunch of lunar paperwork.

Until the moon swallowed its last cat,
he melted fossilized vegetables
and prayed for a plaid taxi home.

Our Moment in the Sun
Bonnie E. Carlson
Fiction

Finally, our time has come. And man, it's been a long
time coming. Seventeen years as nymphs, underground,
feeding on tree roots is a hellova a long time. We hold
the prize for the longest living insects. We built our mud
tubes and bided our time, and the big day has arrived. In
fact, Brood IX has already taken off, scraped and
crawled its way to the surface, broken through, free at
last for our moment in the sun.

When we first emerge from our burrows, we are still
soft and white. Our wings are wet, and we are vulnerable
to being gobbled up by birds, killer wasps, praying
mantises, even racoons and turtles, until we grow our
tough exoskeletons. Fortunately, that doesn't take long.
And besides, there's so many of us, those predators
barely make a dent.

Those of us who survive shed our exoskeletons and
make a beeline for the nearest tree, a place to moult into
our winged adult form, and attach ourselves. Some of us
will become males while others will grow into females.
We're pretty hard to tell apart.

Although we live only weeks as adults, we are
beautiful creatures with bodies as black as ravens; big,
bulging red eyes; and golden-brown membranous wings.
We have an impressive wingspan, up to three inches,
and are big enough to give most human adults pause,
even though we are harmless to humans. Children,
though, have been known to enjoy picking us up.

Fun fact: some humans who have had the audacity to
eat us say we make a crunchy, high- protein snack that
tastes — listen to this — like canned asparagus. We
wouldn't know.

As adults, our sucking mouthparts allow us to drink plant sap. Delicious! But job one — in fact our only job — is to mate. We amorous males yearn to find a mate, to sing, to vibrate the membranes on the sides of our almost hollow abdomens, creating our distinctive cacophonous buzz-saw sound. Can you believe that some of our brethren produce sounds loud enough to cause permanent hearing loss in humans? Our chirping and clicking become the soundtrack of early summer in the South. Some humans say one of us sounds like radio static, but millions? When the boys all get going at the same time, we create quite a racket. Deafening, according to some.

We guys like to hang out in groups and hope females will find our courtship songs to be irresistible. Our favorite time to sing during is the hottest part of the day, and we pride ourselves on being the loudest insects. It's thrilling when we hear the sound of a female clicking her wings to let us know she fancies us. We click our wings back and the mating dance is on. When a lady decides she likes us, we position ourselves back to back and do our thing using our wings to cover us, providing some privacy.

After that, sadly, the quintessential moment we fellows have been waiting seventeen years for, our job is done. Now it's up to our lady friends. They lay up to four hundred eggs on vines and in grooves they make in the tender bark of twigs. Humans get annoyed, incorrectly referring to us as locusts, which we hate. They worry about their crops, their fruit trees.

Not our problem.

It takes a month and a half for those eggs, no bigger than an ant, to grow into nymphs that feed on tasty tree sap before they fall to ground and burrow their way into the soil in search of tree roots. Our forelimbs are so well adapted to underground life, we can build burrows and continue our lifecycle beneath the earth. So begins the next long phase of our life.

If you think that was exciting, wait until next spring when Brood X of magicicada periodicals arrives, billions of our buddies taking to the skies, singing their little hearts out.

Wonderland
Angelica Whitehorne
Fiction

You were supposed to do something, but you have forgotten what. You keep walking around and around the twisted bike paths of your town. You look at the clock, a rabbit runs by, more time is lost. This is your city, it's made of concrete and displaced dreams. The Big Gulp from the gas station sits on the ground with a chewed straw, cigarettes are growing from the field like daisies, receipts from Walmart flicker through the air like turtle doves and everyone keeps nodding off during the motion picture of this two-star town.

You come upon doors and they should lead out because they are doors, but they are all locked with biased trivia questions like
   "How many daughters of single mothers grow up to find loving partners?"
   Or "How many welfare babies make it into grad school?"
   The largest door just says, "Why do you think you are the exception?"
   You almost give up hope, who can answer the rhetorical? But then you see the glass vile labeled ego and you drink and grow and step over the doors which are now the size of popsicle sticks.

On the other side of the doors there is a table of politicians. They are wearing colorful hats and drinking large drinks: a little mix of healthcare, a shot of loan forgiveness, a squeeze of organic lime.
   You stand around the table as they argue and pour sugar over everything and steal each other's mini-

umbrellas, but no one offers you a drink, no one even offers you a seat.

The town representative crawls out of your mouth and smokes a fat pipe, lounging on your tongue, he says, "I have news and it is bad."

"What is it?" you ask

"Bad news, I am, and you are?"

"Alice! No Angelica! I am Angelica!" you say as best you can with a smoking cat on your tongue. You are so glad someone finally asked.

"No, you are bad news," he puffs, and you realize you are and take a drag to forget your names again, the one you came with and the ones others have given you along the way.

You visit the Queen next, who is actually just a screen. Everyone is looking up and staring at her and she becomes angry when you try to look away. She challenges you to a game of Candy Crush and when you beat her she says, "Off with your head," so you crop your photo so it is only your body, and she posts you on the top of the feed so everyone can see and point and count the birth marks on your thighs.

All along and afterward, you feel as though you are supposed to wake to something else, as if you were underwater and should be rising, but morning after morning you get up and this town is all there is.

Blossom
Aisha Malik
Poetry

I stare out the window in the middle of the night
Crying everything but flowers
The weather is beautiful, It's May
And somehow everything seems to blossom
But my womb
The lake gives birth to a new generation of life
Even the rain seems to flourish
The moon seduces the rose
The sun winks at us
Heaven and hell make love
To propel the universe
And I fail to create life
All my life I was told there was only one way for a
woman to blossom
She had to be ripe for the picking
Her lips red from the apple
Only good for sin
My mother was the best sinner
Emulated the one who gave birth to Jesus
sacrificed herself on the altar
So we wouldn't end up on a cross
took her womb and turned it inside out
Why I can't be like her?
Remember God loves sinners
Life is awfully quiet
Without the laughter of a child
Maybe I would not feel so empty
If you did not look at me like I wasn't already home
I was enough
I hold your soul when the skies are shaking
I already give you flowers when the rest of the world
　　　　Dies

Do you still worship my body knowing you won't find God?

Eulogy for the Family Car
Sara Naz Navabi Jordan
Poetry

I long to live my life within walls.
I don't care where we go,
they're taking me
where I need to be.

I long for leather
seats and steel doors.
Sacred leviathan;
I'd go to Stockholm.

I long to be forever
defined, delimited, determinate.
I long for our own brand of dysfunction;
it was ours.

An ache in my acerbic gut
for so much ancient scrap.
Hiss and jeer with your brandished scythes! —
This unhallowed gas guzzler is all I know.

Ghost-shapes and pixelated colours
in my raining rearview.
I am swaddled
in rust.

Mum's Cane Beating
Miracel Uzome Ikechi
Poetry

Coding codes for a cool coda
Calmly crying with a shanty-shanty
Rushed home with a boda-boda
Reached and saw her cany cany

As mum is smiling smiling
As fast my heart is beating beating
Daddy turns my paddy paddy
The fear of mum's cany beating

Silently walking; turned a zigzagger
"About to watch home human junker"
Siblings laughed at the bitter banter
While I turn to a partly panter

Light falling gently gently
Heart beats rises slowly slowly
While I lay alone and lonely
I had to miss the night jolly

Pitter patter of paws on the floor
Applying more moor while I murmur
Silent cries like a murmur
And I woke with a different colour.

A Garden Bench in Early Spring
William Ogden Haynes
Poetry

Walking through the back yard, I gather the scattered
dry sticks from one more winter. I inspect the perennials,
shocked from the cold, everything above ground faded

brown. And as I clip off the dead fronds, I know that
life persists in the bulb beneath. These plants have
many more lives than a cat, and will no doubt outlast
me.

The weeds, often the first to emerge, wait patiently
under the dead autumn leaves to organize their annual
takeover of the garden. Soon, daffodils will be rising

from their beds, and the greening trees will re-form
a canopy over the yard as they have done for decades.
And then there is the garden bench, frail with rust,

riding a downward spiral, waiting for the wire brush
and Rust-oleum, so it can last another season. But
eventually, it will be cast into the street after I am

no more. I'm not a perennial. I never sink into the
ebb and flow of dormancy and regeneration. I am
built more like the bench, always there, through

all the seasons, flourishing for as long as I can,
but steadily deteriorating. For unlike the perennials,
once I leave this life, I will never come back to it again.

What I Should Have Been Saying
Patrick Meeds
Poetry

This morning I woke
to strange marks and bruises
on my limbs and torso.
Hieroglyphs of raised flesh I cannot
decipher. One thing is for certain
something has bitten me
and it will not heal. It will
not stop itching. Two perfectly
symmetrical holes throbbing
in unison with my pulse. I tried
pressing the back of a hot spoon
against the wound but it did not help.
It only served to distracted me
from the fact that I am in love
with the imperfect. A guitar solo
with one bum note. A smile
with one crooked tooth. Finding
one of your eyelashes in my soup.
Learning the true names
of things is now my only goal.
Bear's House, Denali, Tewaaraton.
It will be my new superpower.
It will be better
than my old superpower
which was saying I'm sorry
when I should have been saying
I love you.

Summer Night Sounds
Patrick Meeds
Poetry

The other sound I remember from that night
was someone smashing the windows
in the abandoned Photomat hut.
We were eating ice cream and watching
those two boys, shirtless and sweating, fighting
in the Friendly's parking lot while empty sundae cups
balanced on overflowing garbage cans.
It seemed to be ending when all of the sudden, snap,
a broken elbow. For a moment before he went down, the
boy
just stood there looking at his arm hanging useless,
like it belonged to someone else.
Someone said the smaller boy knew karate and someone
else said someone should have stopped it, but no one
did.
Do you know that an elbow breaking sounds just like
the popping noise a log makes in a campfire?
The gaseous wood alcohol and water trapped inside
heated until they're vaporized
and released.

Ghosts in the House
Peter Obourn
Fiction

"Wine snob," said my sister, Deborah, standing with my refrigerator door open. "You never have any beer." She lifted out a bottle of Meursault and took a swig out of the bottle. "How can you drink this horse piss?"

"Listen to this," I said. I pushed the button on the telephone answering machine and played the message from Aunt Marcia. *Phillip, you cannot sell the house. Call me immediately.*

"Well, that's short and to the point," said Deb. "So what are you going to do?"

"Ignore it," I said. "Mom died more than six months ago. The house is listed. I don't want it. You don't want it. It can't just sit there. Pour me a glass of that."

"Pour it yourself," she said and handed me the bottle. "You have to call her. You always avoid confrontation.[1] That's your whole problem. She's our aunt. We can't ignore her. Either you handle it or I will." She finished the wine in one swallow. "Got any more of this? We'll just pay Aunt Marcia a visit tomorrow. I'll pick you up at noon."

* * *

Aunt Marcia uses her "parlor" only for company, which is a rare event. Most of the time she sits alone in the kitchen, last remodeled in the seventies, in her "house on the hill," which she calls it, except it isn't.[2]

Deb and I sat on Aunt Marcia's chintz sofa, which looks and feels like fabric stretched over plywood with

---

[1] This is a lie. I just don't rush in like a fool.

[2] Actually, it's sort of in a hole.

rocks for throw pillows. Deb had hypocritically worn a dress, so I knew that she was going to do an act. Our aunt was wearing a floral dress, which looked the same as every other dress I've seen on her. Deb says no one can figure out where she buys them. Although it was lunchtime she didn't offer us anything to eat or drink, not even a glass of water, which didn't surprise me. I'd never seen Aunt Marcia eat or drink. She probably thinks it's unladylike to eat in front of others. "I was born there, your mother was born there[3] and lived her entire life there," said Aunt Marcia. "It's our ancestral home."[4]

"Aunt Marcia," I said, "it's a simple matter of necessity. The house can't just sit there."

She started to cry.[5] "It was always understood that it would be in our generation until your mother and I were gone.[6] I can't stand the thought of someone outside the family living there.[7] Can't you do anything, Deborah?" she said.

Deb got up and put her arms around Aunt Marcia. "I wish I could. Mother left all the decisions to him,"[8] she said with a dismissive nod in my direction. "He can do anything he wants. All I get is a little money, which, of

---

[3] Notice she doesn't mention their older brother, my Uncle Mort, who was not a bad guy but had a little trouble with the Securities and Exchange Commission and became *nunc pro tunc nonexistent* as far as Aunt Marcia was concerned.

[4] My grandfather bought the house in 1936 in foreclosure. Three families and the bank had owned it previously. There are five other houses just like it on the street.

[5] Actually, just dabbing her dry eyes with the stiff linen handkerchief she had for the occasion.

[6] Dead.

[7] They might be Puerto Rican or black or Italian or German or Canadian.

[8] Another lie

course, means nothing to me."[9]

Aunt Marcia shook her head. "My little sister was always such a silly fool."

"I'm sorry, Aunt Marcia," I said.

"Well, we all have to do what we have to do, I guess," said Aunt Marcia. "The sad thing is that those people who buy this house are going to have to put up with the ghosts."

Deb and I looked up. "What ghosts?" said Deb.

"Why, the spirits of Mother and Father and my dear sister. They won't leave that house until I'm gone. We all promised each other that."[10]

Deb, who had sat back on the plywood divan, returned to Aunt Marcia and put her arms around her again.[11]

"I understand, Aunt Marcia, of course. Don't worry. We'll take the house off the market immediately," said Deb. "Right, Phil?"

"Deb," I said, "that creates a problem. There are taxes to pay, the lawn to mow and all that kind of stuff."

"Well," said Deb, "look at it this way. What if something happened and someone in the family needed a place to live?"

"What are you talking about?" I said. "Everyone in the family has a place to live."

"Well, I mean, you never know," said Deb. "What if, say, someone just turned up, like, say, Uncle Mort.[12] I expect he's still around somewhere. He's family. He'd have a place to live."

---

[9] Ibid.

[10] At the time Illinois law required Realtors to disclose all ghost sightings. I knew it and Deb knew it, and would Aunt Marcia have brought it up if she didn't know it? Not likely.

[11] This was a world record of hugging Aunt Marcia for Deb, two in one day without retching

[12] See footnote 3 above.

"That's absurd," said Aunt Marcia.

* * *

We walked up the slight slope from the house on the hill to the road. I kicked the loose gravel as hard as I could. "What is the matter with you?" I said. "Uncle Mort? He has to be dead by now. Are you crazy or something?"

Deb looked at me in that superior way she has. "Relax, Phil," she said. "Listen. Probably he *is* dead by now but maybe he isn't, or at least I bet Aunt Marcia doesn't know for sure he isn't. And now, thanks to her, he'll have a place to live, dead or alive."

* * *

The next week I got a call from Aunt Marcia, all sweetness. She wanted me to sell the house — as soon as possible. "Phillip," she said, "I've changed my mind. You know, Deborah came to see me again, and we had a long talk. I feel good about new people moving into the homestead. I hope you find a nice young family, any family."

I said I was pleased.

"I'm sure you are," she said. "I know it's hard for you to sell the house you grew up in to strangers. But we have to move on. I just can't stand the thought of those family ghosts hanging around. So I told them all to shoo and they did."[13]

THE END

---

[13] Blood is thicker than molasses, usually.

Rebecca turns her head
as if listening to the quick darkness

and stands for the smallest moment
to return earrings to the smallest holes

There, casual astonishment
the bedroom where

we've been living together
for each other for so long

she works at one lobe and then the other
while days tumble together in their

smallest gestures little kindled hours
like matches burning out our bodies

the earrings are studs
simple and sharp

When Tenderness Lingers
Bill Wolak
Art

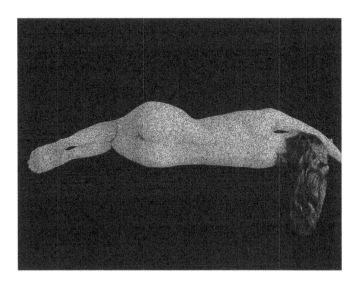

Lavender
Michael R. Lane
Fiction

"Lavender."
 "Eggshell."
 "Lavender."
 "Eggshell."
 "Lavender.
 "Eggshell."

Muriel and Clay stood in the middle of their home office, after a Greek omelet breakfast, still wearing their pajamas, looking around as if checking the room for lurking spiders. The couple had been going back and forth for a month about what color to paint the ceiling and walls. The stalemate had no effect on the rest of their lives. Social, personal and work were all going smoothly considering the Governor ordered quarantine due to the COVID-19 pandemic. Their office had been the most neglected room in the house prior to the quarantine. Sporadically occupied since both preferred performing their paid labor tasks at their places of work.

They were in their fourth year of marriage after a fourteen-month engagement, and two-year dating period. Disagreements were nothing new for the pair. Arguments were far fewer but always passionate. Muriel had researched the effects of colors on a person's mood and behavior. She presented her case to Clay. Explaining how studies had shown, the color lavender encourages a relaxed meditative state. Clay fired back, "This is an office, not a yoga studio."

"This is our home, first and foremost," Muriel retorted. "What's wrong with bringing a sense of tranquility into our place of business?"

"Tranquility and business are not compatible to me," Clay responded. "How about eggshell walls with lavender trim?"

Muriel brushed that idea aside. "Lavender walls with eggshell trim."

The color debate continued. Both agreed either choice would be a big improvement over the drab beige that made the room feel like a tomb.

Muriel's phone rang. It was her doctor. Muriel was expecting her call. Muriel had her yearly physical last week that included blood work. She answered. Moments later Clay's phone rang. It was business. He answered. They stood an unintentional safe social distance apart holding dual conversations. Muriel hung up first.

"Honey," Muriel said appearing stunned. Clay raised a hand as a signal for Muriel to wait a moment while he responded to a question from his caller.

"I'm pregnant."

Clay's phone slipped from his hand crashing onto the hardwood floor. Neither reacted to the accident. Clay slack-jawed, eyes wide with astonishment, dumbfounded expression, gulped before saying to Muriel, "Lavender it is."

The End

Neighborhood Watch
Dylan Morison
Fiction

We, the righteous many of the Neighborhood Watch,
find it necessary to inform you that your family has been
appropriately investigated and deemed exceedingly unfit
for our neighborhood; therefore, we find it unavoidable:
You must be eliminated. Please see below, a detailed
account of our collective grievances:

First, we must address your children, whose
fascination with slugs and efforts at quantifying local
cockroach populations has not gone unnoticed. The
boy's stutter makes the neighborhood children face deep
wells of sadness they cannot understand. Watching him
struggle through basic salutations makes us all
uncomfortable. We couldn't begin to articulate the
collective helplessness and squirmy horror represented
among us. The girl's no better. Her uncanny impressions
of every individual in the neighborhood make us wonder
who's really watching whom? The children can only
grow up to be criminals. This will not be tolerated.

Your husband certainly doesn't seem to care if your
family continues living in this neighborhood. In the past
377 days your family has lived here, your husband has
maintained the lawn exactly seven times. We know. We
counted. Huge vines and bushes over run your home,
there are broken terracotta pots and unfinished mosaics.
There's an algae-choked pond, not to mention the
numerous invasive species your husband insists on
referring to as *Avant-Garde Landscaping: A Botanical
Study in Colonialism*. This is about respect: basic,
neighborly decency. Can't you see our perfectly coiffed
lawns? Our timer-based sprinkler systems? Don't you
ever look at our lawns and then look at yours and then

look back at ours again? One of our informants swears they saw a monkey swinging through the mimosa trees in your front yard, and another swears a black panther was seen prowling through the overgrown grass. Your husband is always laughing. We can hear him blocks away, spoiling our good times while we're hosting our backyard barbeques. *How dare you?*

And so this brings us to you. Oh, *you.* We think you're likely the most dangerous of all. We saw you: naked in the moonlight, arms outstretched. We saw you sneaking out to the rooftop to smoke joints before dinner. We saw you in the grocery store, braless, buying the stinkiest cheese. We don't know why you came here, and we don't know what you want. We must protect our families. It's what we've sworn to do. We're watching you.

Fairy Tale
Trivarna Hariharan
Poetry

While on our way
to a meadow,
my friend & I
caught a pond
rippling with frogs.
They were like
paper-boats flown
by children.
Fugitives hunting
for a home.

We caught them
by their silver-oiled bellies
& ran them into
little-fingered ferns.

But we did not
just leave it at that.

We took care of them
until they were turned
into young princes

by women
seeking
bride-grooms.

What Remains
Trivarna Hariharan
Poetry

Grandma
while crouched on your bed one day,
you tumbled suddenly —
like a door off its feet.
Father lifted you in his arms
like a basket of berries.
Mother & I had not yet reached.

Slowly,
a stream of ants started
garlanding itself around
your body. Small, red ones
that you would always scrape
from the insides of
breadcrumbs.
Look how they hide inside
any hole they find, you would say.

You must be laughing at that now.
Laughing at it,
having seen how everyone —
whether ant eating breadcrumbs,
or people eating ant-eaten breadcrumbs:
all dwindle down to crumbs
themselves.
How gently your body
was flown into the river.
Un-caged as a suitcase
of sandalwood
flowers.
Days after that,
I could not tell sleep from

awakening. I measured
the ropes of time by shoelaces
I had never learnt to tie
on my own.

eggs
Jane Ayres
Poetry

when breaking an egg
the shell fractures in my hand
scattering brown flints into the yolk.

I chase them round the bowl with a teaspoon
scooping out the debris. I usually miss a bit.
fragile and strong

eggs are clever beasts.

when we were children
you cooked us chucky eggs
couldn't stomach them yourself

yet you lovingly cut fingers of white bread
thickly buttered soldiers
to dip in the soft yellow

and push forcefully into the runny yolk
until it rose up over the lip
& dribbled away

childhood fragments leaving sticky mess.

when I look in the mirror
I see your face.
me become you become me.

splinters of maternal love jagged beneath my skin.
the comfort and fear of inevitability
the future foreshadowed.

no more eggs for me.

heartsick
Jane Ayres
Poetry

watching patterns form on glass
you are waving
but I can no longer see

unable to sleep
I listen to foxes singing duets
while you snore beside me

rain falls steadily
you leave
but the world still turns

Lollipops
Shannon Frost Greenstein
Poetry

It has always been lollipops
that break my bad habits.

Lollipops, licking
oral fixation satiated
impulses and compulsions
sublimated into frenetic sucking.

Lollipops
instead of the needle
sliding into a vein
or the nubs of my fingernails
lost to my teeth
or the blade against my skin
because of the overwhelming
self-loathing

Lollipops
watermelon, strawberry, grape
red, pink, purple, never yellow
to keep me alive
and relieve the pressure
that constantly looms
drowning my amygdala
with all of the neurotransmitters
I so desperately crave

Lollipops
to build a life worth living
(in the Linehanian sense)
to keep my husband
and build our family

to better my self and rise above
the trauma that weighs me down

Lollipops
to break bad habits
to stop my sins
to ride the urges
and quiet the voices.

Lollipops
to save my life.

Shoo Flies
Sheldon Birnie
Fiction

The boy wakes me up in the middle of the night.
"Daddy," he'll whisper, crawling into bed next to
me. "I'm scared."
"Come here," I'll say, wrapping the quilt around
him. "Don't worry."
"The room's full of shoo flies," the boy mumbles,
nearly asleep.
Any bug that flies is a 'shoo fly' to the boy — he's
only three — except maybe butterflies and bumblebees.
For his own reasons, he's taken a dislike to the things.
No small wonder. Can't stand them, myself.
"It's OK," I'll shush, as much for his benefit as my
own, wide awake as I am and staring up at the ceiling.
"Just a dream."
In the light of the day, we'll sit at the kitchen table,
eating.
"Ugh," the boy says, waving his milky spoon
through the air in front of him. "Get outta here, shoo
fly."
Sure enough, a little something bobs around above
the bowl of bananas. I'll reach out over the table, slowly,
then smack my palms together. When I open my hands,
I'll show the boy.
"Yuck," he'll say, making a face if I got 'em.
"Rats," if I missed.
When the boy's mother and I first started seeing
each other, she was staying in a studio apartment above
a bakery. Once I started spending the night, I'd wake to a
big fat fly buzzing around my head, alighting on my face
as the early morning sun broke through the blinds. It
disgusted me, but I was head over heels with her. Instead
of suggesting she spend more time at my place — a

rented room in the basement of an old boarding house on the other side of town — I doubled down.

"We should move in together," I blurted one morning, figuring she'd call my bluff.

"For real?" she said instead, grinning big in that way that showed her chipped eye tooth, brown eyes sparkling mischievously. "That'd be fun!"

Fun it was, for a while. We got ourselves a one bedroom apartment in a decent little neighbourhood not far from the university, filled it with furniture from the Good Will, got back into studying once the fall rolled around. Then she got pregnant. After the boy was born, neither of us went back, though we both planned to pick up our studies when time allowed.

Now she's gone. Gone, gone, gone. It's just me and the boy, now. And the shoo flies.

When we're sitting around, the boy and me, the sight of a fat house fly buzzing idiotically against a window sends my skin crawling. I've sent my morning cup of coffee or my evening beverage crashing against the linoleum when startled by the creepy touch of their legs on my skin.

"What's wrong?" the boy will ask, eyes wide with worry.

"Nothing," I'll mutter, stooping to clean up the mess. "Shoo flies."

When I was a boy myself of about eight or nine, I had a little rabbit for a pet. Soft white fur, cornflower blue eyes. She'd put up with just enough cuddling so as to endear herself as a pet, hijinks and all, and not a moment more.

She could get nippy, though, if she set her mind to it. And that's just what she done one early autumn afternoon when I went to bring her inside and out of the Indian summer heat. So I left her to sweat it out there for another hour or two before I brought her in just after dinner. Next morning, I went in to give her a squeeze before heading off to school, but when I picked her up she wheezed in pain and nipped at me again.

"What's up girl?" I started asking, but then I seen just what was up. I dropped her back in her cage with a moan of my own and turned, hollering for my mother. Bugs were crawling all up the back of the bunny, munching the poor thing up alive. My mother took the rabbit to the vet, who put it down, while I stayed home crying, horrified and disgusted.

Later, in the darkness, the boy will be waking me up again soon, with his soft shuffle step and a whimper as he climbs into the big bed.

"There are no shoo flies here," I'll lie with a whisper.

"There," he'll insist, pointing up into the shadows. "The black buzzing things. Shoo flies."

I'll stare up into the far black corners of the room, which does indeed seem to buzz around, like a negative of static on a TV screen. I know it's nothing, the absence of light or something in the shadows, but I don't know how to explain it.

"It's nothing," I'll insist as soothingly as I can manage, while I lay there thinking.

I wish I'd held that rabbit close, that I'd soothed her, at least a little, in that final hour. But I never.

I wish I could have done something, anything, to keep the boy's mother here with us. But I couldn't.

I wish I could keep the shoo flies out of our goddamn apartment, but I can't even do that.

Of course I don't tell my three-year-old son any of this. What use would it be? Where would I even start?

"It's nothing," I'll lie, as much or more for myself than the boy. "Shoo flies."

Furnish, Furnace
Rachel Stemple
Poetry

The severance pay comes late
after the basement flames:

a fire set respectably
by neighborhood watch

when she recognizes
the *both* of us. Two too slimy

millipedes weaved like
it really *is* my genetic makeup.

Royal Turkey
June Levitan
Art

Shattered Illusions
Edward Michael Supranowicz
Art

Opossum
Kensington Canterbury
Fiction

Its body was mangled from the fall.

That, I remember.

I was eight or nine at the time. I can't remember my exact age.

They can be funny like that. Core memories. These crucial moments that shape us as children. The details escape you, but the images stay behind. Festering in your sub-conscious.

I heard something outside.

Four older kids from the neighborhood had jumped the fence into my backyard. They were chasing something. I walked outside and saw them.

They were standing in a circle around this tall dogwood tree that was just starting to bloom. Their heads were all turned upward.

Staring at something.

From behind the branches, it moved. Too large to hide itself.

An opossum; very common near my childhood home in the hills of Georgia. This one was a little fatter than most. It stared down at the boys below; trying to keep itself from being seen. Trying to decide whether or not it was safe up in the tree.

My father was always doing home repairs. Our yard was constantly littered with leftover supplies from failed projects. On the side of our house was a loose pile of bricks.

One of the kids walked over and grabbed one.

He hurled it as high as he could into the branches. It flew through the air, my young eyes following it, and smashed against the trunk of the tree just a few inches shy of its target.

The opossum hissed down at its attackers below.

They laughed in response.

One by one, they ran back and forth between the bricks and the tree. Flinging them with frenzy. Always just missing the animal by inches.

In a panic, the opossum grabbed frantically at the sparse branches above it. Maybe it would be safer up higher. Maybe it just needed to climb. But there was no way up.

It was trapped.

It hunkered down onto the only branch that would support its weight. Doing everything it could to make itself appear small. Occasionally, it would hiss and spit at the boys below, but that seemed to only excite them more.

All of their bricks missed.

Until one didn't.

One brick hit the animal square in the side.

There was a terrible shriek as it fell towards the Earth and I watched it bounce a little as it hit the dirt.

Then, silence.

The boys walked over to see what they had done. Smiling, they stood over their creation.

The opossum was still alive. It tried to move. It struggled to pull its body forward with its front paws. Its back paws lay limp. Its back was broken.

It tried to hiss. To scream one final scream of pain and anger at its murderers, but the attempt was wet, gargled, and barely made it past its throat. Its lungs were slowly filling with blood. So, it just lay there, experiencing the last few moments of its life in agony.

Until one of the boys lifted up his foot and brought it down on the animal's head.

The head flattened against the ground. Its eyes popped loose from their sockets and burst in the open air. Most of its brain matter seeped through its ears. The rest oozed out of the open wound in its skull.

Almost instantly, ants began to crawl over the corpse.

Then, the boys left.

I never saw any of them again. Almost like they weren't even human. Just some vicious species of demon that sprung forth from Hell with the sole intent of killing one opossum.

But they weren't. They were just bored kids. Killing time on a day off.

I'm not sure why I needed so desperately to see the body, but I remember walking up to it. There was something in me, some dark curiosity, that demanded to be satisfied.

The opossum lay motionless. The many injuries, brutal and varied, decorated its body. Its head was black with ants.

At the time, it was the most blood I had ever seen.

Now, I am older. I have seen enough to last a lifetime. But no matter how much pain and death I witness, or how much I cause, I always find myself drawn back to that opossum.

Laying in the yard with its head split open.

Killed for a laugh.

Something moved across its shattered back. Something breathing. A small joey. Barely more than an infant. The opossum had been carrying a passel on its back. That was why it looked so fat before.

The child's siblings were all dead, but somehow it had held on to life.

Injured and pinned down under the corpse of its mother, it was unable to move. Its eyes were just barely starting to form, and as its first sight, it stared at the cruel and unforgiving world around it.

It looked at me, and for a brief moment, we understood each other.

Two children.

Scarred.

Learning about violence at too young of an age.

Then the ants began ripping it into pieces, so it would be easier for them to carry.

Portrait of Mom Giving Birth
Anthony Aguero
Poetry

It is hard to silence a scream
once it's been heard.
Slasher film reeling ad infinitum.
The body at the bottom of a pool
is the only exception.
An epidural seems in conflict
with its own purpose:
pain leads to ease leads to birth.

She talks to her psychiatrist
about my body at the bottom
of a pool in Palm Springs.
Slasher film reeling ad infinitum.
Confesses the epidural
was her most painful experience.
Help me redefine worth as
something less needle
knocking gently against
the spine.

Sometimes it's easier to hear
someone say you've got it right:
the scream becoming a murmur
Slasher film reeling ad infinitum,
but this time at the opening scene
where the pool glistens with
so much hope and summer.
My newborn cries ringing over
and over and over and over.

Lethargic
Anthony Aguero
Poetry

My grandmother no longer owns her home.
Dementia took its grip, clipped her wings,
and now someone in some home carries her.

Anytime I am sad I call my mother and say
Mom, I am sad and I feel like I want to cry
and she's so pragmatic and I am carried.

The first boy I acknowledged to truly love
now lives somewhere in Texas, in that red-
place. That red rushing throughout my body.

My cousin Priscilla pulls me out of a high-
school day and we drive in her white mustang
singing out the window to Bubbly.

Sometimes I listen to Bubbly and sing so loud
it's hard to recognize that I have started to cry
but I am only in an apartment in Los Angeles.

One night I was watching something and I was
struck with a certain type of thirst that water
wasn't capable of quenching and a desert.

I grew up in a desert. A dry plot of land meant
for growing kale, lettuce, carrots and so much
more everyone eats. I touch my skin and crumble.

So I Am Dust
Anthony Aguero
Poetry

And that frightens you
kitten in the pond of things
the way upstairs neighbors
rustling their furniture
forces me to jump in bed
So I am gradual movement
not waiting for a part
the way I toss and turn
attempting to align my spine
just right but nothing is
ever right
So I am dust I am fallen
I have stripped my wings
but I am no martyr
I am just a purr in your throat
waiting to leap out
So I am dust so I am dust
and I fall back into place.

Addiction
Yash Seyedbagheri
Fiction

I spend twelve hours writing, Nan. I can't get off the computer. Remember what happened after that *B*? Dad's monologue?

I know you're doing sisterly duties. Yes, I drink Diet-Pepsi. I have to pick up the pace.

I'm not sad again. I love you, Nan; I just can't slow down.

Horse Race
Will Brooks
Fiction

Always looking to fast-track his position in life, Lyle
had purchased thoroughbred racehorses. He built his
own track in back of the milk barn of his dairy farm, and
his first breeding produced a female horse who, at two
and a half years old, Lyle thought was ready to race, or,
at best, make him a profit.

To see what the filly would do, Lyle and his buddy
Terry loaded up and drove to a track outside Sterling,
Oklahoma. The hope was the filly would place in the
race and be noticed by a potential investor.

After arriving, they went to registration, where they
paid their entrance fee and found a jockey who agreed to
ride the horse for payment, up front. The Mexican
jockey hardly spoke a lick of English, but was the right
price for Lyle, cheap.

"Who saddles my horse?" Lyle asked the man
operating the registration desk.

"You do."

"Where?"

"In that barn, right there."

Lyle looked at the barn, then back at the man, not
sure he had heard him right.

"I saddle my own horse, by myself, in that barn?"

"Yep," said the man, already moving to the next
patron.

Lyle turned and grabbed Terry by the arm,
whispering, "Come on, Terry, this must be the
crookedest track in the country."

Inside the barn, Terry watched while Lyle bridled
and saddled the horse. Now, Lyle was practiced enough
in life to know that evolutions in living didn't happen
quickly. They took time and hard work. But with aid you

might skip certain steps and accelerate fate. This was just such a moment.

"Okay, Terry. Hold on to her bridle."

"Why?" Terry asked as he watched Lyle fill a syringe from a glass vial. "What's that?"

"B-12. I'm gonna charge her battery. You just hold on to her."

Terry grabbed on either side of the bridle, facing the horse so they were eye to eye. Lyle administered the shot. Immediately, the horse's eyes rolled into the back of her head, briefly leaving only the whites before her irises popped back forward, pupils dilated. The filly's head bobbed and her right leg twitched as if someone had hit a switch. Then hell busted. She reared up, loosening Terry's grip momentarily.

"Hold on to her! Stand your ground! Don't be a coward!" Lyle yelled encouragingly, but far enough away he wouldn't get kicked or mauled.

Terry kept his grip, leading the horse outside by spinning the mare's head in circles while leading her toward the door. The noise of neighing and kicking drew spectators who came to see the rodeo. In the crowd was the Mexican jockey, who took one look at the horse and stated:

"No ride! No ride!"

"Yes ride! Yes ride! You've been paid, you son of a bitch," Lyle replied.

Meanwhile, Terry was white-knuckled, holding on for all he was worth, and stammered, "Well, somebody do something!"

"No ride!" the jockey yelled again.

"Yes, ride, you coward. You've been paid," Lyle yelled while placing a fresh twenty from his pocket into the jockey's hand. Finding new inspiration through the green-faced Andrew Jackson, the jockey mounted the horse, reminding Lyle of news footage he had seen of a monkey climbing a tree during a hurricane.

Terry now had his right arm wrapped around the horse's nose in a headlock move. The filly lifted his feet inches off the ground every time she jerked her head as they made their way to the track. At the edge of the track, the jockey lost his nerve again and started to dismount.

"No go!"

"Yes, you will go!"

Terry, straining to keep his hold on the animal, mistook *you will go* for *let her go,* and loosed his grip. The filly, feeling the release, bolted.

Dodging the advances by third-party people to corral her toward the starting gate, the mare took off backward around the track. The jockey just held on for the ride as the mare rounded the track with explosive speed.

Back at the starting gate, the mare cannonballed through a chute in the starting gate. The gates slammed shut behind her; simultaneously the other handlers spooked her into turning and crowded her into a chute just as the buzzer sounded for the start. She took a short lead and stopped, stock-still, out of juice.

"She couldn't even run fast enough to scatter her own shit," Lyle shouted, throwing off his hat and stomping it in a fit.

The jockey jumped off the horse like a man would a sinking ship. Terry ran out and grabbed the horse's reins, pulling to lead her off the track. Refusing to budge, she leaned in the opposite direction of Terry's conduct. After twenty minutes of the horse not budging, the groundskeeper brought out a tractor and pushed the filly into Lyle's stock trailer he had managed to back to the edge of the track. Lyle and Terry started home with the filly in tow, Lyle not stopping to ponder any chance inquiries about the filly.

Annoyance
Arianna Sebo
Poetry

popping my temples
tripping my veins
making my heart explode inside
implosion
reverse fireworks
I want to submerge my head in
a tank of boiling water
burning my flesh
and scorching my brain
maybe that would stop me from
thinking
boiled eyeballs
a delicacy
for fat frogs
and dragonflies

On The Highway
Arianna Sebo
Poetry

Exciting events on the horizon
no more planning needed
only driving to and from
destinations
Soaring along the highway
catching birds in flight off guard
deer whistle whirling
singing at the top of my lungs
cats howling
coyotes yelping
the light of the moon casting
shadows over my SUV
no one in sight
but us people
in our high-powered vehicles
on vacation

living in an hourglass
David Eldridge
Poetry

Peering out. Hoping for the glass to break.

Longing to explore the world. To make a difference
Worried time will expire. That it will suffocate us.
Drown us in experience.
Without an opportunity to truly experience.

Sand accumulating.

love's foil
Eileen Kwan
Poetry

i. She was a lot of good things — all right besides
him

Where his toes once found the shadowed floorboards
at the breath of dawn, his fingers now woke to her soft
sighs and sweet breath, the lingering supermarket
shampoo still tracing her hair. Finding the flesh of her
waist and the whispers of her dark hair the way he had
looked for the sun on cloudy mornings, he drew her
close and felt the gaze of bashful clouds peeking through
the glass.

Sunday evenings in the city's backyard became the
story he had read from the windows and the movie he
had watched from the landing. Holding the arm of the
bench — just a film companion — he watched: the boy
with blocky legs who danced a slanted tumble for the
shy flowers and the humming bees; the woman who
sang of cakes and pretty days as she painted and
breathed colors beneath the willow; the dog and squirrel
which were locked in a siblings' bicker and the never-
ending daze of ring-around-the-rosie. In the distance, on
the edge of the page and in the corner of the screen sat a
man, a smiling man who held the arm of a bench as he
looked at her, the kiss on a baby's forehead and the rush
of soles against dew.

The cold chills of lonely nights were wet drapes that
bled into his skin, choking thoughts that vomited hard
sputters and dry tears. Resurfacing when the moon
called, his eyes ran red and his heart fell cold, gone. Yet,
she was there. And she waited. With her candle in one
palm and the other outstretched, she sat there with him.
Through the frost that decorated the tips of his words
and the thaw of the bitterly sugared pond. She sat.

ii. He ran. Ripping through the velvet curtains of thickets and wrinkled brick walls, he slashed in a madman's haze; it was a sweep of the soul and the glimpse of gold's brilliance — but not at all. Flowers choke on petal gowns and soulless beetles, running through and in the stem's neck of honey. They sit without the valleys. Their friends. I watched as they walked away with the wind, the opening of a promise and the sweep of ending credits. The beetles had said the river was prettier. I listened as they cried, drowning in Alice's tunnel and hands crushing bones flushed clean of flesh. The silence hung as the laundry of linen and solitary do. As the sun cried the blush of first love and the soft crunch of early summer's sticky melons, he held hands with the mourning doves and her sister Socorros. The branches laid in a bed of colored skins as they danced one last time. It was a waltz for the lonesome and the wails that fumble in echoed staccatos, running after arpeggios that already know the way while knowing. They sat with me through the pounding murmurs and the gold light of street lamps, and I sat with them in the gold light of Universe's tycoons and waterfall pangs. As they jumped, dipped, skipped, and hopped — pit, pat, stop — pavement steps thrummed with a light heart. They hummed a soft tune, rocking the trees and blowing bubbles that held his body. Hers in his. In soft plumes of giddy pixies and tilting pirouettes of excelling love, she spun with the angels. She fell over and over and over and each time his love caught her.

Chaos.

iii. As her eyelashes pricked the spinning wheel, she tasted the sweet bullet of cottage fires. The stillness of nothing and absolute. Sleeping Beauty missed it, and God missed her.

vinyl
Christine Brooks
Poetry

I wanted to
march in anger
stand in protest and
kneel in prayer

for the many

the so many I could not count
the so many I did not even know
the so many that never counted
not at all   not to those doing
the counting anyway

all I could do though
was reach back   the way a sad
song reaches back
across the vinyl to console
us in
pained solidarity because
no one ever listens to a sad song
when they're happy

perspective
Christine Brooks
Poetry

the pavement under my feet led the way down the steep
mountainside
past the empty bus stop
towards both the bush & the
surf

the sand under my feet, blown in from the Tasman Sea
crunched under my hot pink sneakers & the sun on my
face
made me look Maori as my Jolly host family joked

drunken Tui birds dangled in many of the kowhai trees
that I walked past early this morning
when my small New England neighborhood was still
dreaming & never noticed the long white cloud that
carried me back
to New Zealand

The Soul of the Boots
Sara Pisak
Nonfiction

Standing at attention by the cottage's fireplace, I wait
patiently for your orders to march through the day's
events. While at the fireplace, I admire the fine
craftsmanship of the cut stonework I helped you lay by
hand. When you pick me up and carry me along, it is
easy to see your hands are worn with callouses. The
lines tell not of future fortunes but of past constructions.
  You lace me up, pulling the reins tight through the
eyelets. A double-knotted bow is my headband. When
you trod my soles on the rocky path, I teeter along, like
your nine-year-old granddaughter, careful not to lose my
grip on the limestone ledge. I see you hold her hand as
she pretends the stones are a balance beam. Descending
the stones, leaving light impressions on the mossy grass,
I take the lead. Now, I don't worry about tumbling over
the steep trail, and neither do the two of you, because we
have reached the well-worn path leading to the dock.
Eager to hear the anthem of the whistling hinges of the
dock, you hoist Sara on your shoulders, and I heel ball-
change onto the boards. From the pressure, the dock
gives and springs back against the water jolting the three
of us into the air.
  We have trodden countless steps from the shed to
the dock and back again, bringing all the supplies needed
to clean the boat, fix the motor, and stock the boat with
fishing supplies for our after-dinner fishing trip. Your
broad shoulders carry the bulk of items, while her little
hands carry the yellow Mister Twister lures, the Shur
Strike crab lures, and the wrenches. Sara is infatuated
with your tackle box. Too heavy for her to lift, she waits
for you to place the tackle box in the boat before she
continuously opens and closes the latch, changing her

mind on which of your antique lures will lead to the perfect catch. She can't decide between the Bass Oreno orange spotted lure or the Pikie Minnow, that is, until the Lucky 13 lure catches her eye. I enjoy when she tags along on our adventures, but with each step, I like to think you couldn't have done it without my support.

My steel toes clack as I maneuver around the motor trying to help you reach the propeller. Suddenly, tar-black grease plops like an ink splatter atop my laces, not necessarily egg on my face. The blob is proof of a job well done, but if we track grease through the cottage, Irene will be livid — remember the time you and Sara crouched in the silt of the river bed watching the beaver build his dam and then forgot to check my treads, which later smeared thick mud on the carpet. One last rotation of the wing nut and you drop the motor back into the water with a splash. Closer to the water's edge, I am soaked with cool water, even on my tongue, before your flannel shirt is drizzled with the clear, crystal water.

If I had known this would have been our last summer at the lake together, I would have memorized everything. How the grass felt beneath the waffle grid, what birds or wildlife joined us on our walks, the items we salvaged, and everything you said while we were together. But I didn't know. I guess no one really knew you wouldn't make the annual trip the following June and that these would be the last outings the three of us would share. I wouldn't see the outdoors the same way: you teaching Sara how to start the motor, and how to swim – your synchronized freestyle strokes bouncing both of you back and forth like a pinball between the sheltering shores of the cove walls. This would be the last summer of her bounding along after us, chasing us through the thick trees and standing next to me each morning at the fireplace waiting for you to begin the day's projects. For years, my leather skin has been worn and tattered, but like you, I was still able to fight through and finish the job. I would have guessed I would have gone first. You had such a big heart; I wasn't the only one who thought it would never give out.

But here I sit, where you placed me each night and picked me up each morning: by the fireplace. When the family returns next summer, will they decide to leave me by the fireplace? That way, when they see your boots all scuffed, worn, and tattered, it will seem as if you will be back to pick me up and begin our work again.

in which the book has a dream or three
Glenn Ingersoll
Fiction

In this dream I am lying on a railroad tie and it is
shaking as the train comes down from the mountain. I
wonder if the engineer will read me. Perhaps the train
will screech to a stop, the engineer will get out, crunch
across the gravel. He will reach down, pluck me from
where I am lying and brush the dust from my cover with
his canvas-gloved hand. Then he will look into me. He
will look into me the way he looks down the line, seeing
the track stitching the landscape together, looking at how
the way has been laid out for him and is always the same
and he is always the same and nothing changes but the
weather and what gets in the way. The vibrations of the
coming train move me. A bird throws its silhouette
against the white sky. The train is shaking the earth.
Where is it? The sky remains white, and I try to imagine
myself its child. I could grow up to be a white white sky.

In this dream I am burning. I have been tossed onto a
bonfire. The books and magazines heaped up here have
been soaked with kerosene and throw giant flames high
into the air. A small girl steps out of the crowd which
has been taunting the books and throwing on new ones.
She climbs up the pile with enviable balance. It doesn't
look like she's having any trouble. I am midway to the
top and it looks like she is going to step right past me
and go on up, but she stops. She leans over and looks at
my title page, my cover having already curled back and
fallen off. She picks me up, and my personal garden of
kerosene-fed flames brightens her soft face. She reads a
paragraph, then a second paragraph, a flicker of
amusement touches her lips. She steps over to an atlas,
rides it down the pile and steps through the circle of

chanting people. It is dark away from the pile, but she can read by my fire. She started in the middle so now she turns to the first page, serious about reading a book. "Welcome," she reads, exposing the word that had been hiding so well. "Yes, please enter." She walks on through the streets. As she finishes a page it flares briefly then takes flight, breaking into ash and sparks.

In this dream I don't fit on the shelf. I am too tall. I have been turned so my spine faces up. Even so the shelf above won't let me stand straight. The books are not tight on this shelf, so I have room to rest at an angle. But I still stick out into the hall. When people pass they have to turn sideways to get by. Someone wants to look inside me. He pulls me from my place, but I am so long I hit the opposite wall before I am free of the other books. In order to get me out he's going to have to remove the other books and swivel me around. But once he has he is surprised to find I am now snug up against the back of the bookcase and the hall's opposite wall, jammed in, in fact. He pushes on me and I bend. He is afraid of breaking my spine. I know he won't. He can push and pry all he likes.

Tim Finally
Mary Fontana
Poetry

made his way through the Rosary
for the first time at Connie's
funeral. Five decades and change
they'd had together and all that time
she'd been the one to know her way
by heart down the beads, knew
how to gather in that grace
so he didn't have to. He broke horses,
rattled the tractor clean off the hill.
Now his fingers fumble on wood
but still he drives, drives homeward
toward Amen, his great back heaving,
half-thinking he'll see her momentarily
as he always used to at day's end,
standing with water in the lit doorway.

At the Bridge above the Tide
Keith Moul
Poetry

The late ferry bobs, awaits its sailing time
with rocking equanimity, perhaps captain
and crew aware with every trip that lovers
anticipate their passions' motions, boarding
as hedge than love exhausted in satisfaction.

Oh to be cold-blooded as the frothy winter
tide tumbles at me exposed on the bridge,
cavorting freely among these very waves.

Warm blood faces inhospitable immersion,
as the local gull buffets wind, never to watch
me flounder in the bay, but to set its cocked
maw for any meal. I dream of pleasing sun,
its warmth, so harbor personnel will not be
tasked with heavy surf as they try to hook
and bundle my lifeless body for its terminal
indignity and identification at the morgue.

Colorado
E A Schubert
Fiction

Blood comes off better in cold water, she tells me. I beat my arms against my favorite laundry stone like a soiled apron, watch the red ribbons loosen from my skin and disperse rapidly into the creek. I look at Annie; she hasn't a drop on her, but her eyes are wild and flickering and the ridges of sweat on her lip and on her brow shine like pearls in the moonlight. Her sleeves are pushed up almost to her shoulders, and I can see how strong her forearms are, rippling with muscles and still very brown from her work in the big garden. I remember the first day I came to work here. Cora had shown me to my tiny room at the back of the huge farmhouse. It was autumn, the frosts had appeared, but snow had yet to fall. I saw Annie out the window as we passed through the long, windowed corridor, hauling fat yellow pumpkins through mud like they weighed nothing, her head bare and her black braid swinging, her brown boots shiny like beetles. I stopped to watch her. She left very deep footprints.

"That's our Anne," Cora had said, "Strong as a man, keeps the whole garden herself." Then in a low, conspiratorial voice, Cora had told me how Annie's husband had gone missing just three months into their marriage. The entire town of Peacher's Mill had gossiped over the case with abandon, until the wretched man's body washed up drowned on the banks of the big river, not a week before I arrived. *Suicide,* Cora had whispered and given me a knowing look.

Drowning must have been cleaner. Easy for someone so strong. *You're like me,* Annie said to me the day after her husband's funeral, her eyes shining. I wanted it to be true, but I was frightened, and she

impatient. It was already the start of my second winter at
the farm when she told me unequivocally that it was
time, as I carried stained bedsheets through the garden to
the creek, watching her drive wooden stakes into the
frozen ground.
"You know what you must do. If you still want it."
Annie's eyes did not meet my own. I could see beads of
cold sweat gathering on her dirty neck. She struck her
mallet too hard, and the stake split down the middle.
    The pitchfork was a messy affair, a desperate, rushed
job out in the pasture, the lowing of the cows drowning
my husband's groans. What else was I to do when I saw
him this evening, out in the pasture with that slack-jawed
smile and a hand stuck lazily into his trousers, waiting
for me to call him to supper? I could only speak Annie's
words to myself, over and over; I could see only blood.
    I needed her strength to drag his body into the
shadow of the cypress trees, hidden behind curtains of
Spanish moss. I needed her to tell me what to do: to
direct my clumsy scullery hands on the spade, to
encourage me through the hours of digging, to push the
cold dense mound of soil and worms back over him. I
don't remember walking to the creek, I don't remember
pushing up my gingham sleeves, wet with his blood –
but now I feel the icy water shock my skin and it's like a
lightning strike in a nearby field: suddenly I smell the
fire and sense the fizzing in the air. We are free. Annie
comes beside me.
    "Be still," she says, and I realize I am trembling. I
feel her hands at the small of my back. She unties my
apron, reaches around my shoulders to unpin it from my
breast. It slips away like the blood. She unbuttons my
dress with warm, strong fingers, undressing me firmly
and tenderly. It's so different from my wedding night,
when Amos clumsily pulled my dress off over my head

before subjecting me to his limp, sweating body. She stands above me on the bank.

"Get in," she says, and I am suddenly submerged in the creek above my waist; the cold is like knives. She steps in after me, doesn't even flinch.

"Tell me again," I say, feeling like the cold could put me to sleep, "Tell me about it."

Her cupped hands warm the water as she rinses the blood and dirt from my torso, wipes my skin with her own wet skirt. The foul matter washes away easily, flowing west, away from the farm, away from our husbands' graves, their money already in our pockets.

"Colorado," she says. She unbraids my hair and rinses the sweat from it. She kisses the nape of my neck and I can't feel the cold anymore. "We're going to see the mountains," she whispers.

"See the mountains," I echo, and with another pass of her hands, I am clean.

Contributor Bios

Awósùsì Olúwábùkúnmí Abraham
Awósùsì Olúwábùkúnmí Abraham lives in Ìbàdàn,
Nigeria. He has gained a myriad of rejection letters but
still submits. Most times, admire the girl in a picture. He
can be reached on email via awosusib@gmail.com.

Anthony Aguero
Anthony Aguero is a queer writer in Los Angeles, CA.
His work has appeared, or will appear, in the Bangalore
Review, 2River View, The Acentos Review, The Temz
Review, Rhino Poetry, Cathexis Northwest Press, 14
Poems, and others.

Jane Ayres
Based in the UK, I finished my MA Creative Writing
last year at the grand age of 57 and am fond of porridge
with chocolate melted on top. When I was 40 I wanted to
be Buffy the Vampire Slayer. Last Christmas I had a job
in Santa's Grotto as an elf — for two whole days.

Brett Biebel
Brett Biebel teaches writing and literature at Augustana
College in Rock Island, IL. His (mostly very) short
fiction has appeared or is forthcoming in Chautauqua,
the minnesota review, The Masters Review, Emrys
Journal, and elsewhere. 48 Blitz, his debut story
collection, will be published in December 2020 by
Split/Lip Press.

Sheldon Birnie
Sheldon Birnie is a writer, dad, and beer league hockey
player living in Winnipeg, Manitoba, Canada. He rides a
bike and hasn't had a hair cut in going on three years. He
can be found lurking online @badguybirnie.

George Briggs
George Briggs is a high school teacher from Rhode
Island. His work has appeared in Isacoustic*, Ghost City
Review, Turnpike Magazine, and elsewhere.

Christine Brooks
Christine Brooks is a graduate of Western New England
University with her B.A. in Literature and her M.F.A.
from Bay Path University in Creative Nonfiction. Her
poem, the price, is in the October issue of The Cabinet
of Heed and her poems, life and I Don't Believe, are in
the fall issue of Door Is a Jar. Two poems, friends and
demons are in the January 2020 issue of Cathexis
Northwest Press and her poem, communion, is in the
January 2020 issue of Pub House Books. Her series of
vignettes, Small Packages, was named a semifinalist at
Gazing Grain Press in August 2018. Her essay, What I
Learned from Being Accidentally Celibate for Five
Years was featured in HuffPost, MSN, Yahoo and Daily
Mail UK in April 2019. Her first book of poems, The
Cigar Box Poems, was released in February 2020. Her
second, beyond the paneling, is due out in early 2021.

Will Brooks
I currently work for my family's propane company. I
love working with my hands and enjoy many outdoor
activities, hunting being my favorite pastime. I live on a
large farm in a house that was built with lumber
harvested and milled right on the farm over sixty years
ago. My work has appeared or is forthcoming in Hawai'i
Pacific Review, Evening Street Review, Pencil Box
Press, State of the Ozarks, Ignatian Literary Review,
Critical Pass Review, Stirring: A Literary Collection,
and The Penmen Review.

Kensington Canterbury
I am an active duty Sailor in the United States Navy, and currently reside in San Diego with my wife Maria and our two children.

Bonnie E. Carlson
Bonnie E. Carlson lives and writes amidst the saguaros and chollas in the Sonoran Desert, letting her pets be the boss of her. Right now it's too darn hot to hike, alas.

Linda Conroy
Linda Conroy is a retired social worker who likes to observe people in their environment and write about the behaviors that make us human. She enjoys singing, playing the fiddle and other instruments, and reading beautiful words.

David Eldridge
While living in New Orleans in the 1990s, David Eldridge wrote a great deal of poetry. But, for about a 20-year period, he had little inspiration to write. While staying-at-home due to Covid-19, he began writing with much fervor and, through that writing, discovered a renewed soul.

Michael Farfel
Michael Farfel lives and writes out of Salt Lake City, Utah. His work can be found with Juked, Trampset, X-R-A-Y Lit, Bone Parade and in his forthcoming novel with Montag Press. MichaelFarfel.com.

Mary Fontana
I am a scientist and writer living in Seattle, Washington. Despite several degrees in biology I cannot seem to keep houseplants or pet fish alive, and this year's crop of quarantine tomatoes is also looking iffy. However, my

two young children are thriving (though perpetually covered in mud).

Shannon Frost Greenstein
Shannon Frost Greenstein is the author of 'More.', a forthcoming poetry collection from Wild Pressed Books. She is an avid fan of Mount Everest, Nietzsche, and her two darling children, and is ostensibly attempting to acquire another cat, despite the objections of her husband, at this very moment. Shannon comes up when you Google her.

Trivarna Hariharan
Trivarna Hariharan is a writer and pianist based in India. Besides writing — she loves to cook, meditate and watch the birds that visit her veranda.

William Ogden Haynes
William Ogden Haynes is a poet and author of short fiction from Alabama who was born in Michigan. He has published seven collections of poetry (Points of Interest, Uncommon Pursuits, Remnants, Stories in Stained Glass, Carvings, Going South and Contemplations) and one book of short stories (Youthful Indiscretions) all available on Amazon.com. Approximately 200 of his poems and short stories have appeared in literary journals and his work is frequently anthologized. http://www.williamogdenhaynes.com

Miracle Uzoma Ikechi
Am from Abia state, Nigeria. A poet who let's my feelings flow through my pen.

Glenn Ingersoll
Glenn Ingersoll works for the public library in Berkeley, California where he hosts Clearly Meant, a reading &

interview series. The multi-volume prose poem 'Thousand' (Mel C Thompson Publishing) is available from Amazon; and as an ebook from Smashwords. He keeps two blogs, LoveSettlement and Dare I Read. Other excerpts from Autobiography of a Book have appeared in Inverse Journal (as fiction), E-ratio (as poetry) and Caveat Lector (as essay).

Sara Naz Navabi Jordan
I am an Iranian-Canadian mother of two young girls, living in Vancouver, Canada. When I'm not busy trying (and mostly failing) at pinterest-mom crafts on the playroom floor, I'm working an office job, or escaping to my bedroom to write.

Eileen Kwan
Eileen Kwan is a high school student. Her only personality trait is her love for Korean pop (K-pop). This piece was inspired by the K-pop song "your eyes tell" by BTS, and thus it is recommended that the song is played in the background to enhance the reading experience!

Michael R. Lane
Michael R. Lane has studied literature and creative writing at Point Park University, Sonoma State University and Portland State University. His fiction has appeared in Door Is A Jar (Summer 2020, Issue 15), The Hungry Chimera, THEMA Literary Journal, Inwood Indiana, Spindrift, African Voices Magazine, Potluck Mag, Taj Mahal Review and a few others. Michael is the author of four published novels, two short story collections and three collections of poetry. Learn more about Michael at www.michaelrlane.com.

June Levitan
June Levitan is a retired teacher from the South Bronx.
Now she takes photos for fun.

Aisha Malik
Aisha Malik is an emerging writer. Her poems have been
featured in 3 Moon Publishing and Dream Walking. She
hopes to publish a book one day.

Patrick Meeds
Patrick Meeds lives and works in Syracuse, NY and
studies writing at The Downtown Writer's Center at the
Syracuse YMCA. He has been previously published in
Stone Canoe literary journal, the New Ohio Review,
Tupelo Quarterly, the Atticus Review, Whiskey Island,
and is forthcoming in East by Northeast Literary
Magazine.

Mark J. Mitchell
Mark J. Mitchell was born in Chicago and grew up in
southern California. He is very fond of baseball, Louis
Aragon, Miles Davis, Kafka and Dante. He lives in San
Francisco with his wife, the activist and documentarian,
Joan Juster where he made his marginal living pointing
out pretty things. Now, like everyone else, he's
unemployed. A meager online presence can be found at
https://www.facebook.com/MarkJMitchellwriter/

Dylan Morison
Dylan Morison is a fiction writer currently based out of
Baltimore, Maryland. A graduate student by day and a
line cook by night, Dylan is pursuing her MFA in
Creative Writing from Vermont College of Fine Arts.
She has an adorable dog named Bunny.

Keith Moul
Keith Moul writes poems and takes photos, doing both for more than 50 years. He concentrates on empirical moments in time, recognizing that the world will be somewhat different at the same place that today inspires him. His work appears around the world. Besides his reprint of his 2012 book Beautiful Agitation, also scheduled for 2020 release is New and Selected Poems: Bones Molder, Words Hold.
http://poemsphothosmoul.blogspot.com/

Zach Murphy
Zach Murphy is a Hawaii-born writer with a background in cinema. His stories have appeared in Peculiars Magazine, Ellipsis Zine, Emerge Literary Journal, The Bitchin' Kitsch, Ghost City Review, Lotus-eater, Crêpe & Penn, WINK, Drunk Monkeys, Door Is A Jar, and Yellow Medicine Review. He lives with his wonderful wife Kelly in St. Paul, Minnesota.

Rami Obeid
Rami Obeid is a writer from Mississauga, Ontario, Canada. He writes poems on the subway and listens to Gypsy Jazz in his spare time.

Peter Obourn
My work is forthcoming or has appeared in Blue Lake Review, Bombay Gin, CQ (California Quarterly), Crack the Spine, descant, Evening Street Review, Forge, Gastronomica, Griffin, Hawaii Pacific Review, Inkwell, Kestrel, The Legendary, Limestone, The Madison Review, New Orleans Review, North Atlantic Review, North Dakota Quarterly, Oyez Review, PANK, Quiddity Literary Journal, Red Wheelbarrow Literary Magazine, Riddle Fence, The Round, Saint Ann's Review, SNReview, Spillway, Stickman Review, Switchback,

Valparaiso Fiction Review, Verdad, Viral Cat, Voices de la Luna, Wild Violet, The Write Room, and The Blueline Anthology 2004. My short story "Morgan the Plumber," which appeared in North Dakota Quarterly, has been nominated for a Pushcart Prize.

Sara Pisak
Sara's hobbies include reading, fishing, swimming, and making stained-glass. When not writing, Sara can be found spending time with her family and friends. You can follow her writing adventures on Twitter @SaraPisak10.

Heather Robinson
Heather Robinson is a writer of fiction and non-fiction from Fairfield, Connecticut. She's drawn to dark comedy, satire, and quirky characters who speak their mind or do the unexpected.

Anthony Salandy
Anthony is a mixed-race poet & writer who enjoys writing about the impact of humanity on nature, postmodernism, and existentialism. Anthony travels frequently and has spent most of his life in Kuwait jostling between the UK & America. Anthony has 1 published chapbook entitled 'The Great Northern Journey'. Twitter/Instagram: @anthony64120

Rosie Sandler
Rosie Sandler lives in Essex, England, where she leads creative writing workshops, writes novels and poetry and wears bright colours in the hope of making people smile.

Sally Sandler
At once transcendent and accessible, "A Column of Smoke" gives overdue voice to Sandler's generation of

Baby Boomers and their elders. She illuminates their
shared concerns over the passage of time and fading
idealism, the death of parents, and loss of the
environment, while maintaining hope for wisdom yet to
come.

E A Schubert
E A Schubert is twenty-three and lives in Tennessee
with her partner and their sixteen or seventeen plants.
She engages in bird-watching, collage, and playing the
piano. She also enjoys identifying wild mushrooms and
brings her field guide everywhere she goes.

Arianna Sebo
Arianna Sebo (she/her) is a queer poet and writer living
in Southern Alberta with her husband, pug, and five cats.
Their home is brimming with cat posts, pet beds, fur,
and love. She received her B.A. in philosophy from the
University of Calgary, working in the field of law to
feed her family and writing poetry to feed her
philosophical soul. Her poetry can be found in The
Writer's Club at Grey Thoughts, Kissing Dynamite,
Front Porch Review, and Lucky Jefferson. Follow her at
AriannaSebo.com and @AriannaSebo on Twitter and
Instagram.

Yash Seyedbagheri
Yash Seyedbagheri is a graduate of Colorado State
University's MFA program in fiction. Yash's work is
forthcoming or has been published in WestWard
Quarterly, Café Lit, and Ariel Chart, among others

Rachel Stemple
Rachel Stempel (she/they) is a queer Jewish poet and
MFA candidate at Adelphi University whose work has

been recognized by their nemesis, Billy Collins. Sauteed
onions remind them of larvae.

Edward Michael Supranowicz
Edward Michael Supranowicz has had artwork and
poems published in the US and other countries. Both
sides of his family worked in the coalmines and steel
mills of Appalachia.

Angelica Whitehorne
By day Angelica writes for the Development department
of a refugee organization in New York. By night she
writes her poetry and stories with her 10 plants as
backdrop and her future on her tongue.

Bill Wolak
Bill Wolak is a poet, collage artist, and photographer
who has just published his eighteenth book of poetry
entitled All the Wind's Unfinished Kisses with Ekstasis
Editions. His collages and photographs have appeared as
cover art for such magazines as Phoebe, Harbinger
Asylum, Baldhip Magazine, Barfly Poetry Magazine,
Ragazine, Cardinal Sins, Pithead Chapel, The Wire's
Dream, Thirteen Ways Magazine, Phantom Kangaroo,
Rathalla Review, Free Lit Magazine, The Magnolia
Review, Typehouse Magazine, and Flare Magazine.

Submission Guidelines

Door Is A Jar Magazine is looking for well-crafted poetry, fiction, nonfiction, drama and artwork for our print and digital publication. Please read over these submission guidelines carefully before submitting any work.

Our magazine features new artists and writers and works that are accessible for all readers. Please look at our current and archived issues before submitting your work. Works that are confusing, abstract, or unnecessarily fancy will not be considered.

We only accept new, unpublished work. If you have posted something to your website or social media, this counts as being published.

Contributors can submit to multiple categories; however, only submit once to each category until you have received our decision about your piece.

Upload your submissions to Submittable with the category you are submitting to and your first and last name as the filename. Within the cover letter please include your full name, contact info, and 3-sentence bio.

We accept simultaneous submissions; however, please notify us immediately if a piece is accepted elsewhere. We reserve first initial publishing rights and then all rights revert back to the author. We do not pay contributors at this time.

For more information please visit doorisajarmagazine.net

Made in the USA
Las Vegas, NV
10 February 2021

17528584R00056